milly johnson

Milly Johnson is the *Sunday Times* bestselling author of many novels about friendship, family, love, betrayal, community, good food, and that little bit of magic in life that sometimes visits those who are not expecting it. Milly writes for her local newspaper and often appears on radio and TV. She is patron of several charities, including Yorkshire Cat Rescue and The Well at the Core.

Her publishers call her 'The Queen of Feel-Good Fiction', and together they are aiming to spread as much joy as possible with every book published. Find out more at MillyJohnson.co.uk or follow her on Twitter @MillyJohnson.

milly johnson

The *Little Dreams* of Lara Cliffe

**SIMON &
SCHUSTER**

London · New York · Sydney · Toronto · New Delhi

A CBS COMPANY

First published in Great Britain by Simon & Schuster UK Ltd, 2020
A CBS COMPANY

Copyright © Millytheink Limited, 2020

The right of Milly Johnson to be identified as author
of this work has been asserted in accordance with the
Copyright, Designs and Patents Act, 1988.

1 3 5 7 9 10 8 6 4 2

Simon & Schuster UK Ltd
1st Floor
222 Gray's Inn Road
London WC1X 8HB

Simon & Schuster Australia, Sydney
Simon & Schuster India, New Delhi

www.simonandschuster.co.uk
www.simonandschuster.com.au
www.simonandschuster.co.in

A CIP catalogue record for this book
is available from the British Library

Paperback ISBN: 978-1-4711-8620-2
eBook ISBN: 978-1-4711-8621-9

This book is a work of fiction. Names, characters, places
and incidents are either a product of the author's imagination or are
used fictitiously. Any resemblance to actual people living or dead,
events or locales is entirely coincidental.

Typeset in Stone Serif by M Rules
Printed and bound by CPI Group (UK) Ltd, Croydon, CR0 4YY

MIX
Paper from
responsible sources
FSC® C020471

To all the Lara Cliffes out there . . .

What would life be if we had no courage to attempt anything?

—Vincent Van Gogh

Part I

Hull to Rotterdam

Chapter 1

The Hen Party Ladies

'So do you want tea or coffee?' Lara asked Pip, who was staring hard at the menu. From the look on her face, it was as if she was deciding between life and death.

'I don't fancy tea or coffee. I'm feeling a bit seasick.'

'What? We're still in Hull. We don't set off for another two hours,' Vicky chuckled.

'I know, but my brain is telling my stomach that we're on a ferry and it thinks we're moving,' groaned Pip.

Pip, Vicky, Jo and Lara. Four friends who had known each other since school were about to sail to Holland for Lara's hen party. They would sleep on the ferry, spend a day in Amsterdam, sleep on the ferry, then go home. A mini holiday three weeks before the wedding. It had been Pip who suggested they choose Amsterdam.

'Since when have you been seasick?' Lara asked Pip, thinking that Pip did look pale.

'Since I had the twins. I think pregnancy changed my DNA. Put me on a plane or a boat and I feel sick. I was even ill on a tram in Blackpool, and we only went from the North end to the South. I'm okay with cars and buses though.' She smiled weakly, as if that helped. It didn't much.

'Why didn't you say this to me before, Pip?' said Lara. 'We could have gone somewhere else. I didn't know you hated travelling across the sea so much.'

'I don't. I want to like it and I hoped I'd be okay. Plus I know how much you wanted to go to Amsterdam for your hen party. And we can only get there by going across some water, unless we all swam, and I'm rubbish at swimming as you know.'

Pip was truly hopeless at swimming. She could not float in water. In fact, she had half-drowned in school aged thirteen. She had been trying to dive for a brick dropped in the bottom of a pool in order to get a swimming badge. Mr Fenton, the hunky young PE teacher, had to jump in to rescue her.

Nine years later she had bumped into him in a pub in town and asked him if he recognised her. He hadn't, but when prompted, said that he remembered Pip Ellis as 'that prat in pigtails'. They had laughed about it. Then he'd asked her if she wanted a drink. Then he asked for her mobile number. They were married within two years of their first date.

Pip opened her mouth to say she would have a mint tea, when Jo spoke up: 'What are we doing? This is a hen party. Why are we in Costa choosing coffees when we should be in the bar having some Prosecco? Let's start the party NOW. Come on, ladies. We're wasting time.'

They began walking away from the coffee shop, not really knowing where to go, when Vicky spotted a map of the ferry fixed to the wall. It had been drawn as if someone with a very large saw had cut the ship in half from end to end. There was a red spot in the middle and the words 'You Are Here' next to it.

'Okay, so there's Costa and there's the self-service buffet, and there's the Reef Bistro on this floor. Now, if we go up a floor there are two bars. Left to the Moonlight or right to the Jolly Sailor,' said Lara. They all agreed that the Jolly Sailor sounded the best fun. They were all going to sail, and they were all going to be jolly. If anyone deserved a jolly hen party it was Lara. And they were all going to make sure she had it.

They had met in school and had stayed friends ever since. Vicky and Lara first met aged four in nursery. One of Lara's first memories was fighting with Vicky over who was to wear the Snow White dress in the play box. They met Pip and Jo in junior school aged ten, when their classes joined up for PE. Now, they were all thirty-seven and the years between had been filled with mostly laughter, some tears, but above all a deep and wonderful friendship. They had stuck together through good times and bad and a lot of boys and men.

Now, though, they were all settled. Jo and her husband Benny were barristers who liked travelling too much to have children. Pip – who was now a teacher herself – and Jed Fenton had twins five years ago. Vicky – the first of them all to be married – had had a big fat Greek wedding to Adonis, who was a chef. She helped to run the family Greek restaurant, Zorba's, and they had four children who all took after their father in looks. They were tall with olive skin and dark hair, not short and blonde like their mum.

What those three had in common was that they were very happily married, and now Lara – at last – was going to be too. Her friends were delighted for her, because Lara's heart had been broken more times than any of them could count. If there was a useless man to be found, Lara's heart would find him and fall in love with him.

But three years ago, Lara met Freddie Elmtree. Pip, Vicky, Jo and Lara were having dinner together in Zorba's and were sitting next to a table where a lively gang of men were having a Christmas get-together. Freddie Elmtree was one of them. He turned around and tapped Lara on the shoulder asking to borrow some salt, and that's where it all started.

Her friends worried because Freddie was a huge man with tattoos and a shaved head, who looked as if he had just broken out of prison using that head to break the wall down. But Freddie Elmtree was as strong and solid as his name. He was a builder with his own business, own house, own car and his own lonely heart that needed the company of a good woman. He adored Lara. He treated her like a princess, and her friends could not understand why it had taken her so long to agree to marry him.

Or rather, they did understand. It was all the fault of Lara's ex – Danny Belfont. Her first and worst love. He broke Lara's heart into a million pieces and it had never quite managed to heal itself.

Danny was the love of her young life. He had

a head full of big dreams about becoming a rock star. He was a very talented guitarist, and he and Lara bonded over a shared love of music. He promised Lara the world ... and then, three weeks before their wedding, he dumped her for another woman – Sammy King. She'd gone to the same school as them all but was in the year below. Sammy had dreams about becoming the next Madonna. Dreams as big as Danny's dreams about becoming the next Jimi Hendrix.

Her friends were there for Lara when all that happened, but she was in a bad state for a long time. She went into another relationship too quickly, and it was a disaster. Then another – also a disaster. Then another ... But 'Steady Freddie' Elmtree was the real deal – a good, kind man who treated Lara as she deserved to be treated.

Danny Belfont had stripped away all her confidence. Freddie Elmtree gave her confidence back to her. He made her value herself as she used to do in the old days, before Danny Belfont and his guitar blew into her life. Freddie Elmtree told her that no one would ever value her if she didn't value herself. And the message hit home loud and clear. At long last.

Chapter 2

The First Evening Aboard

In the Jolly Sailor bar, Vicky lifted up her long, slim glass of Prosecco and chinked it against the other three, which were also raised and waiting for her to make a toast.

'Miss Lara Cliffe, may this hen do be as jolly as the rest of your life is going to be as Mrs Lara Elmtree. *Yamas*, as my husband would say.'

'Yamas,' said the other three in a bright echo of the Greek 'cheers' before sipping at their drinks.

Lara smiled then. She would be very happy with Freddie Elmtree because he was the sweetest man on the planet. He had told her that whatever sort of wedding she wanted, she would have it. All he asked in return was that she pick the hymn 'Love Divine', because it was his mum's favourite and she wouldn't be there to see her son get married. She'd died long before he had met Lara.

Lara had no plans to be greedy though. She didn't see the point in spending as much on a wedding gown as some people earned in a year. She found her dream dress in a shop in Leeds after trying on hundreds of them – or at least that's what it felt like.

Her friends had gone with her to help her choose and offer their styling services. Lara had tried on frilly dresses and plain dresses. Dresses so big they would have filled half the church, fancy dresses that cost a fortune and dresses that made her look like a cake. In the end, they had all decided that the one that looked best was a classy white satin one with a long train. It suited her tall, slim frame. She would wear a sparkly tiara in her long, dark hair and carry her favourite flowers.

The service was to be held in a lovely old church and, afterwards, seventy of their friends and family would go to the charming hotel next door to eat a five-course meal. It was the sort of wedding Lara had always wanted. So why was it that she had the feeling something wasn't quite right? It was as if she was looking at a finished jigsaw puzzle with no missing pieces, yet the picture did not look as it should do and she couldn't work out why. She didn't mention it to her friends. They would have said she had last-minute nerves, wedding jitters, but Lara knew it was more than that.

*

They were on their second glass of Prosecco when Vicky looked out of the window and said, 'We're moving.'

'Oh,' said Pip glumly, as if mentally waving goodbye to the safe, still dockside.

'Let's go and eat,' Lara suggested. Apart from taking Pip's mind off being at sea, she was also really hungry.

'Good idea, I'm starving,' said Vicky, who was always starving. It was a good job that she enjoyed going to the gym so much, because her life involved a lot of eating. Her husband Adonis's family was large and merry, and there were a lot of family get-togethers over wonderful home-cooked Greek food.

'We can go to the buffet and serve ourselves, or there's the bistro where we will be served by someone else. Which do you fancy?' asked Lara.

'Are you really asking us that, Lara?' Jo replied. 'We're going to dine in style tonight. I'm not being crushed in a crowd at a buffet for anyone. Reef Bistro, here we come.'

As they were leaving the bar, they heard a voice from the stage. A woman in tight, ripped jeans, a big-hair black wig and very high heels had just walked on. Behind her was a drummer, settling into his seat, and to her side a guitarist with long, rock-star hair.

'Hello, everyone. We are Stardust, your entertainment for the evening. Do please join us,' the woman said.

The guitarist strummed a chord and a cold shiver travelled down Lara's spine. Danny Belfont always played a chord exactly like that when he first went onstage.

'Let's kick off with a little Beatles' number. You might know it. It's called, quite simply, "Help".'

Stardust began to perform. They were a group to be heard in the background, but not really to be listened to. Lara wondered if any of the three musicians on the stage had shared Danny's dream of playing to packed stadiums. And if they still hoped for a shot at stardom while playing to travellers between Hull and Rotterdam, who wouldn't even remember their name by breakfast the next morning.

In the Reef Bistro, Pip was already starting to realise that having the full three courses was a mistake. It felt good, eating the mushrooms in a cream sauce for a starter. Then the fillet steak for a main course, and cheesecake for dessert, because eating stopped her brain from thinking about how much the ship was swaying. Now, all that food was sitting in her stomach, and she was sure that her body had no plans to do anything with it other than just to let it stay there.

'You okay, Pip?' said Vicky.

'Yep. Totally fine.' She tried to smile but it was clear that she wasn't feeling as well as she pretended. Despite the two seasickness tablets she'd taken with her dinner.

The ship was rocking more than they'd expected. Then the waiter had told them to be careful while walking around that evening as high winds were expected.

'Let's go back to the bar,' suggested Jo. 'We can finish off our drinks in there and listen to the band for a bit.' She yawned then and chuckled. 'Assuming I can stay awake long enough to get there.'

The Jolly Sailor bar was very popular that night. Probably because it was in the middle of the ferry and wouldn't rock as much as places near the ends, such as the Moonlight bar, which was right at the back of the ship. Luckily, as the four of them walked in, a group of six people was getting up to leave and Vicky moved in fast to grab the seats and the table.

Stardust were making their way offstage. The female singer said that they were taking a break, but would be back with more songs shortly. She strutted off with the confidence of someone who saw Beyoncé whenever she looked in the mirror, thought Lara.

As if reading her thoughts, Jo said, 'Who do you think that singer sees when she looks in the mirror? Taylor Swift? Adele?'

'Well, you need confidence to stand up on a stage and sing,' replied Lara, before drinking the last of her red wine.

'Talent would help as well.' Jo laughed. 'I could do a better job, and that says it all.'

'Don't you miss it, Lara?' asked Vicky. 'Singing?'

'Not one bit,' said Lara.

'You were so good,' put in Jo.

'Better than good, you were brilliant,' added Vicky. 'Remember that concert we did at school in the fifth form? I mean, we all knew you could sing a bit but – wow – you were amazing. Everyone stood up to clap at the end.' She started to trill 'I Don't Know How to Love Him' and Jo stuck her fingers in her ears.

'Stop, you sound like a cat in pain!'

'Oy, cheeky.'

Pip stood up. 'I'm sorry to be a party pooper, girls, but I have to go to bed. Do you mind, Lara?'

'No, of course not,' she replied. 'Go sleep. I don't want you to stay up for the sake of it. Get to bed and be fresh for tomorrow.'

'I'll come with you,' said Jo, draining her glass. 'I didn't sleep well last night. I was too excited about this trip. I think the sea air is working its magic on me. See you in the morning, girls. Meet us in Costa at eight. Don't forget to put your clock forward an hour.'

'Night, you two,' said Lara as Pip and Jo walked off together.

'Remember the days when sleep was the enemy?' laughed Vicky. 'I hated going to bed. Sleep was a waste of time. Now my bed is like heaven. In a couple of years, we'll be putting our teeth in a glass and walking with sticks.'

'Ah, but in a couple of years we'll be forty, and life will begin all over again,' said Lara, wagging her finger.

'I think that I can stay up long enough to be tempted by a toffee vodka. What do you fancy, Lara?'

'Ooh, I think I'm tempted to try one as well.' Lara reached into her bag for her purse before Vicky stopped her.

'Put that away, lady. Freddie gave me cash to buy all the drinks and food. I'm under strict instructions not to let you pay for a single thing.'

Lara smiled. That was just what her fiancé would do. He was the most caring man she had ever met. She was so lucky to have found him and she really wished she could get rid of whatever was niggling her. Or even work out what it was, so she could deal with it. Nothing should be clouding her happiness. She had everything she had ever wanted. So why was she feeling as if something nasty was about to jump out and give her a shock she wasn't ready for?

There was movement on the stage. It seemed that Stardust had had their break and were about to start their next set. The drummer came out first. He didn't look very excited about being there, as if it was a boring job rather than a passion to play drums.

The singer followed. She had a different wig on now, blonde and curly like Dolly Parton's hair. She'd changed her clothes too and was wearing black leather trousers, black fingerless gloves and a very tight white top buttoned down at the front to show off plenty of boob. She reminded Lara of someone, although she couldn't think who. She didn't know anyone who walked around with massive hair and inch-long false eyelashes.

Then the guitarist wandered onto the stage and played that one chord, just as he had earlier. Lara's eyes snapped away from the singer and to him. She swallowed hard. *No, it couldn't be.* She studied him: the lean, tall frame that fitted denim jeans as if they had been invented just for him, the long, rock-star hair that framed his face like a pair of curtains. It was a face that once had the power to make her heart do cartwheels inside her chest wall. It couldn't be him, her brain was telling her. It was impossible. But it was him. A blast from the past. The guitarist was Danny Belfont.

Chapter 3

A Blast from the Past

The last time Lara had seen Danny Belfont he had been standing in her mother's kitchen doorway. His hair had been a lion's mane of golden curls falling past his shoulders. His jeans had been on the sexy side of tatty and clinging to his slim hips. His beautiful blue eyes had been turned towards the floor as he told her that he couldn't marry her, that he was sorry. Minutes later, her mother ran in screaming like Mel Gibson in *Braveheart*, attacked him with a wet mop and drove him out of the house. Out of her life. That was fifteen years ago. And though she had tried not to think about him since, he had crept into her thoughts thousands of times as if he had a home in her brain.

Onstage, the guitarist raised his head and the years fell away. The face was thinner – and so was the hair – but there was no mistaking those eyes. His blond locks had faded, but his eyes were as bright and blue as they ever were. Lara felt something hurt inside her, like an old pain that had suddenly stirred into life and become active again.

'Sorry I was so long. I had to wait ages at the bar,' said Vicky, plonking herself down next to Lara. 'I bet you thought I'd got lost . . .' Her voice trailed off as she took in the expression on Lara's face. 'What's up, Lara? You look as if you've seen a ghost.'

'I was just daydreaming about the wedding and all I've got to do before it,' lied Lara. She forced out a false smile. The one thing she didn't want to do was let Vicky notice that it was Danny Belfont onstage. Vicky was likely to leap up there and take over from where her mother and her mop left off.

That was nothing compared to what she would do to the singer, because Lara had worked out who she was. No wonder she looked familiar. She might have lost half her body weight, had a boob job and buried her face under a ton of make-up, but the singer was clearly Sammy King. She who had stepped into Lara's shoes in the band and slid next to Lara's boyfriend in bed.

'The boat is moving a bit, isn't it? I think, if it's okay with you, Lara, I'll make this one my last drink.' Vicky gave a pained smile. 'I know this looks bad, me being the chief bridesmaid and all, but . . .'

Lara cut her off. 'Don't be silly.'

'What?'

'I SAID, DON'T BE SILLY,' Lara said again but more loudly.

Now that Lara had seen it was Danny and Sammy, she couldn't un-see them. She wished she hadn't worked out who they were. She was only glad that Vicky had her back to the stage.

'We should have gone to the other bar, I can barely hear you talk for that racket,' said Vicky with a tut, thumbing behind her. 'Whoever booked them must have been let down by someone good at the last minute.'

The truth of it was that she was right. Stardust, as a group, were rubbish. The drummer looked as if he wanted to be anywhere but on that stage. And the singer hit one good note in every ten. The guitarist's skills were wasted playing basic chords that any kid could play after one music lesson.

'I can't wait to see the Anne Frank house tomorrow,' said Vicky. 'One of our chefs went and said it was so much bigger than she thought.' She yawned then. 'Sorry.'

Lara smiled. Even though the four of them had been best friends since school, she was probably a little closer to Vicky than to the others. They were the noisy ones. Jo and Pip had never been sent out of the classroom for talking when they shouldn't have. But Vicky and Lara had been loads of times.

Out of them all, Vicky was the most clever,

though she didn't go to university like her parents had wanted her to. She was happy to cook for a living. She took a job in a newly opened Greek restaurant outside town and, after a week, fell in love with the owner's son. Vicky found her place in life helping to run Zorba's and being a mum. This was the girl who'd once told Lara, 'I never want kids – they're horrible little things.'

'I can't keep awake,' said Vicky, yawning yet again. 'And to think I used to be a party animal.'

'You go back to the cabin,' said Lara. 'I'll follow you in a bit.'

'I'm not leaving you by yourself in a bar, Lara.'

'No, really. I shan't be all that long. I just want to sit here and think for half an hour.'

'How can you think with that din?' Vicky laughed. 'But okay, if that's what you want. I'll see you soon.'

'It is. I'm not ready for bed just yet. I'm too excited, I think.'

'You can finish off my vodka,' said Vicky. 'I'm too tired to drink it – and I don't think I've ever said that before in my life.' And with that, she left.

Now Lara was free to watch Stardust on her own. This wasn't a good thing. She was on her hen do, and yet her eyes were fixed on the man she had loved so much that she had never got over him. Not fully. The first time he kissed her, he almost took her breath away.

'Take my breath awaayyy-yyyeee,' Sammy King sang, and the man on the next table made a face. 'I wish someone would take her breath away,' he said loudly before his wife told him to shush and asked, 'Was it Berlin that used to sing this, Dave?'

'Yes, and I wish she were in Berlin and not on this boat busting my eardrums,' he replied.

That should be you up there onstage with him, not her, said a voice in Lara's head which she wished would shut up.

Lara willed Danny Belfont to lift up his head and spot her in the crowd. He wasn't lifting his head much at all. He was staring at the floor as if embarrassed at being there strumming basic chords that any idiot could play. He must feel like a giant, bouncy dog on a short lead, thought Lara.

'Thank you,' said Sammy at the end of the song. A few people clapped – more of a slow clap than a fast one. Then Danny lifted his head. Lara's heart stopped beating for a second. As if he sensed her staring at him, Danny's eyes turned to hers, locked with hers. It was only for a second at most, but it felt so much longer. The drummer counted in the next song by knocking his drumsticks together, jolting Danny back to the job in hand, but Lara knew he had seen her.

She tried to guess what he might be thinking now, because he surely had to be thinking something. Maybe about the moment when they were first introduced. He grunted a hello before telling her she didn't look like a singer, but like someone who worked in an office. Or when he asked her to marry him one winter night after a gig, when the sky was flooded with stars. Maybe about the time when she lost her voice and a girl called Sammy King, who sang in another band, offered to step in so they wouldn't have to cancel important bookings. Maybe about the moment when Lara's mother hit him with her mop and he ran away dripping wet. Maybe, though, just maybe, he was thinking that he'd seen a woman, who looked like someone from his past whose name he couldn't quite recall.

Lara had been out with a lot of boys and men in her life, but there were only two that she could ever say had really stamped themselves on her heart. Freddie was one and Danny was the other. Her friends always said that she picked the wrong men because she was always trying to replace Danny, and what a mistake that was. They were so happy when she told them that she had fallen in love with a man who was as different from Danny Belfont as it was possible to be. Someone kind, caring, gentle, a man to trust – and not a selfish tosser.

'Wow the ship is rocking and rolling tonight, isn't it?' said Sammy into the mike. She was putting on an air of being cheerful. But Lara could tell that her smile was fake and hiding that something was wrong. She looked like Pip trying to cover up the fact that she was very close to being sick.

'Take it away, boys,' Sammy went on, as if she were playing the O2 arena with Queen behind her. The drummer drummed, Danny strummed, Sammy opened her mouth to sing and then closed it again. The boat rose on a giant swell and people in the bar made 'ooh' noises. Then Sammy King ran for the exit, but not before she had thrown up over the curtains at the side of the stage.

Someone cheered and clapped at the singer's misfortune. The drummer didn't seem to know what to do, but decided that maybe this was a good excuse for him to leave as well. Only Danny Belfont stayed. He stepped to centre stage and spoke into the mike.

'Hello,' he said. 'Sorry about that, everyone. Well …' He played that one chord again and Lara's heart responded with a kick. 'Erm … rather than us leave you with the image of Sammy running offstage like that, I'd like to play us out properly with a song I wrote a few years ago. It's called simply … "The Girl That Got Away".'

'Sounds like he's an unlucky serial killer,' laughed the loud man on the next table, but Lara didn't laugh. She couldn't shift her eyes away from Danny. With the stage all to himself, he began to play properly, like the true artist that he was. His fingers moved expertly over the guitar strings and his soft, smoky voice began to sing. The crowd carried on talking, laughing, drinking. Lara felt as if she alone were listening.

'... The years have helped me see
The girl that got away
Was the only one for me ...'

Lara gulped. Danny was looking right at her as he sang.

'I was a fool to let her go
Is all I have to say
My dreams were hers and hers were mine
The girl that got away.'

Danny was desperate for stardom, and he was sure that his music and Lara's singing would help them find it. And she'd wanted him to have it so much. Was this song about her? Was that what he thought – that she had deserted him? Suddenly she felt stupidly sad and had to blink hard to push tears back down to wherever they were stored.

His voice had got better with age. He had a classic rock-star voice – rough around the edges but capable of so much emotion. He belonged in a different league to a crap group like Stardust. There was no one in this large room who could know how clever and talented Danny was – not from watching him perform tonight. He played the final chords. The song ended. Danny said, 'Thank you very much' and walked offstage to a rumble of polite applause.

Well that was that then, Lara supposed. There was nothing more to hang around in the bar for. She sipped at the last of the toffee vodka. It was a shot really, but it was far too nice to drink fast. She hoped it would make her sleep, because her head was sparking with images of the past. She stood to go but someone put two glasses of wine on the table in front of her.

'I wasn't sure if you were still a white-wine girl, but I thought if you weren't, maybe you could fling it in my face. Hello again, Lara.'

Chapter 4

An Old Flame Burns

Danny Belfont was standing there. Lara's legs lost all their strength. She sat down before she fell down.

'Danny.'

He sat on the chair next to her.

'What a surprise,' said Lara, at the same time as Danny said, 'What a shock.' They both smiled. The ice had been broken.

'What are you doing here?' said Danny. 'Well, I mean, apart from going to Rotterdam.'

'I'm on a mini holiday,' said Lara, wondering why she didn't say that she was on her hen do. 'With friends, but I'm the last one standing.'

'Seasick?'

'Two of them. One of them has four kids and I expect she's just catching up on some lost sleep.' He didn't ask which friend of hers that was. He wouldn't have believed that Mad Vicky Porter would ever have become a 'big fat Greek mama'.

Danny's blue eyes were fixed on hers and his mouth was still curved into a smile. 'It's so good to see you,' he said, and Lara felt his smile travel all the way down to her heart. She really should not be feeling that smile there. It was wrong with a capital 'W'.

'So ...' Lara started to say, without knowing where that sentence was going. She took a polite sip of wine, even though she hadn't drunk white wine for years. Not since she and Danny had split up, and she'd got totally legless on it, and had never been able to face it again. 'So ... you're still playing then.'

'If you can call it that,' said Danny. 'I'm hardly the headline act at the London Palladium. But it's a living. What about you? Did you ever change your mind and start singing again?'

I sing all the time, Lara wanted to say. She sang when she was in the car, hanging out washing, in the bath, but she knew that wasn't what he meant.

'No,' she said.

'What a waste.'

Lara wished she had a penny for every time someone had said that. Freddie never did though. He understood. No point in doing something if it makes you unhappy, he'd said to her when she'd told him about her musical career.

Her teachers at school, her friends, her parents, even people she barely knew who'd heard her sing just the once, had said she must follow a career in music. She must not waste her talent. She was stupid if she did, they told her. How lucky was she to have a gift like that.

So she replied to an ad in the paper – 'Band looking for female singer'. She got the job. Then the band split, and she and Danny formed a duo called Laradan (oh how corny!). Together they were going to make the world sit up and notice them. It had been music that brought her and Danny together. And it had been music that had split them apart.

A cleaner had arrived onstage and was doing his best to sponge the mess from the curtain.

'I didn't recognise Sammy at first. She's changed a lot,' said Lara.

'Maybe in looks,' he replied. 'She's still the same inside.'

He didn't say it as if it was a compliment.

'Are you still together?' asked Lara.

'On and off,' said Danny. 'Probably off now, since it was me who took this gig on until Christmas. She hates boats.'

'I could tell that, from the way she vomited all over the stage.' Lara couldn't resist saying it.

'Yep.' Danny sighed, as if he knew what sort of ear-bashing he was going to get later.

Fifteen years ago, when Lara's throat got better, Sammy didn't want to leave. Danny suggested they form a trio, and Lara had been pushed into agreeing. It was clear that Sammy saw herself as the new lead singer, even though her voice wasn't strong. She was bossy and a pain in the backside, and she didn't want to share centre stage but to own it outright. Lara should have said, 'It's her or me.' But instead she left the group, and then Danny left her life.

'How are your mum and dad?' asked Danny. 'Your mum still handy with a mop?' He grinned and Lara grinned along with him.

'She had her seventieth birthday last month. She and Dad went skiing for the first time. She had a big health scare three years ago, and made a bucket list. They've been on a helicopter over the Grand Canyon, on a gondola in Venice, ridden on elephants in India. As bucket lists go, it's been a very expensive one.'

'Am I on that list?' asked Danny. 'As in "Kill Danny Belfont"?'

'That was all a long time ago now,' said Lara. 'She's forgotten.' Which was a total lie because Lara's mother still called him 'that scruffy bumhole you were once engaged to'.

He pointed to her left hand, which was cupping her glass.

'Nice sparkly ring you have there.'

'Yes, it is, isn't it?'

'So you're engaged again?'

'Yes.'

'Is he a musician?'

Yes, he's Jon Bon Jovi, she wanted to say.

'He loves music, but he's not a musician.' Freddie was tone-deaf, which didn't stop him belting out tunes as often as he could. They always sang together in the car. Their favourite song was 'Paradise by the Dashboard Light' and Freddie relished being Meatloaf for the length of the tune. He made her laugh as, in the middle of the song, he would do his very bad Elvis Presley impression.

He made her laugh a lot. Right from the very first second, when he tapped her on the shoulder and asked if he could borrow the salt pot from their table. As she handed it over, she dropped it on his leg, and he said he was going to have her arrested for *a-salt*.

'He's a builder. He has his own company,' Lara went on.

'And what do you do?'

'Accounts.'

Danny scrunched up his face, as if doing accounts was the worst job in the world, which it would be to him.

'Accounts.' The tone of his voice matched his face.

Lara shrugged her shoulders. 'I like it.'

'Sounds boring as hell,' Danny sighed. 'Oh

come on, Lara. You aren't meant to be working in an office and you know it. You should be singing on a stage. With me. We were so good together. Perfect – we were perfect. I don't know why it went wrong. Can you remember that place in Leeds where the crowd stood up for us at the end? And they wouldn't let us go without singing another five songs?'

Lara let herself mentally sink back to that time. Sixteen years ago. Had it felt good to be clapped and cheered and prized by so many people? Oh boy – yes it had. She'd been on top of the world. Not because of the crowd, but because she knew how happy it made Danny.

Danny's hands reached forward and took hers.

'It really is so good to see you. Did you know I was on the boat?'

'No, of course not.'

'Then it must be fate. What else could it be?' He smiled, and she remembered when that smile warmed her heart like a bonfire. It had tortured her, when they split up, to think that he would be smiling at Sammy King like that from then on. Danny Belfont had stolen the sun from her heart.

His hands squeezed hers and it felt wrong, and yet at the same time so familiar. As if her body had never forgotten his touch. She slid her hands from his just as the drummer appeared at the side of the stage, scanning the crowd.

'I think you're wanted,' said Lara, nodding her head towards him.

'When are you coming back on the ferry?' said Danny, waving at him.

'Tomorrow night. We're only spending the day in Amsterdam.'

'Meet me. Same time. This bar. Let's have a proper talk.' He scratched his head. 'You being here has happened for a reason. You don't know how much I've been thinking about you recently, and then you turning up ... It's meant to be. You've made my head spin, Lara. Please.'

No, Danny. We have nothing to say to each other, said her head.

'Okay,' said her heart. 'I'll be here.'

It was her heart that had control of her voice.

The sea was rough that night. Lara felt every wave for the next hour, at least, as she lay in her bunk, her brain fizzing with activity. On the other bunk, Vicky snored softly, rocked by the ship's motion as if she were in a giant cradle.

Lara wasn't feeling very proud that here she was, three weeks before her wedding to Freddie, with a head full of her ex-boyfriend who dumped her three weeks before their wedding. Seeing Danny had screwed with her mind, and opened up a sealed box of memories that she had stored away because it hurt her to think of them.

She could remember the first time she ever saw him as if it were only an hour ago. He was tuning his guitar, looking lean and moody in faded denim jeans, a Pink Floyd T-shirt, and that cloud of fair, messy hair. He'd totally ignored her at first, apart from that line about looking as if she worked in an office. Only when she'd opened her mouth to sing had he taken notice of her. And then he had told the rest of the band not to even think of taking on anyone else.

Afterwards, they went for a drink in an old man's pub around the corner where he told her that he wanted to reach the top, move to America, buy a big car, a ranch, be rich and famous, make records. She wanted that too, at the start – because everyone had told her that someone with her talent must want it all. The first time he kissed her, she thought her heart would burst open, because the joy inside it was too big to hold. For three mad years, he was her everything. Then he had been her nothing and it had half-killed her.

Lara fell to sleep with her head full of Danny Belfont, as if he had never been out of her thoughts. And that lovely song played in her head – 'The Girl That Got Away'. She hadn't got away; he had thrown her away like unwanted rubbish.

Part II

Rotterdam to Amsterdam

Chapter 5

The Happy Pancake

'Morning!' Lara was woken by Vicky shaking her. 'Blinking heck, Lara, I thought you were dead for a minute. How could you have slept through all those bing-bong tannoy calls? They've been going off since six. Get up, you lazy sod. We're in Rotterdam and I need a coffee.'

Lara opened her eyes and, for a split second, she expected to see Vicky's teenage bedroom and not the cabin of the boat. She used to stay over at Vicky's house a lot when she was young. The four of them were always camping out in each other's bedrooms, but Vicky had the full top floor of their house to herself. And she had her own wonderful pink bathroom.

Lara always wanted a bathroom to herself and she was to get her wish. She and Freddie had designed their own new home, which would be ready for them to move into by Christmas. As a surprise for her, he'd altered the plans to make sure that she had both her own dressing room and her own bathroom. Then she could decorate it in pink with unicorns if she wanted to, he'd teased.

'Here, this is your costume for today,' said Vicky, and passed her a carrier bag. Inside it was a headband with two hens' heads on wire springs fastened to it, and a T-shirt, with a picture of a hen's head, and giant pink lettering: 'LARA'S HEN DO – I'M THE HEN'.

'You. Are. Joking,' Lara said.

'No, I'm not. You're lucky you got this. You have no idea what Pip wanted you to wear.'

Fifteen minutes later, Lara was showered, dressed, wearing her headband and walking towards the meeting place in Costa with Vicky, who was wearing her own headband and 'LARA'S HEN DO – CHIEF BRIDESMAID' T-shirt.

Pip was feeling much better now that the boat had stopped moving. She and Jo had slept well, and had coffees waiting for the others. They could have had breakfast on board, but decided to have something in Amsterdam instead. A friend of Jo's had told her about a little café that sold great food. It was called the Happy Pancake. In Holland pancakes were something special, Jo's friend told her.

The bus journey from Rotterdam to Amsterdam

took a little over an hour. Vicky sat with Pip in her 'LARA'S HEN DO – BEST-LOOKING BRIDESMAID' T-shirt. Behind them sat Lara and Jo, in her 'LARA'S HEN DO – CLASSIEST BRIDESMAID' T-shirt. She was too. Jo oozed magical classy vibes. She even made her hen-do costume look like something Coco Chanel had designed.

Jo was feeling guilty that Lara ended up sitting in the bar by herself last night.

'I wanted to,' Lara laughed. 'I wasn't ready for bed and it was nice sitting there, sipping a toffee vodka.'

'Toffee vodka? That sounds yummy,' said Jo.

'The singer threw up over the curtains.'

'No way!' Jo gasped. 'How awful, feeling crap but still having to go onstage and sing.'

Lara remembered then, waiting in the wings to go onstage and dreading it. Someone saying to her, *Once you get out there, you'll feel amazing.* She hadn't. All she wanted was to do what she had to and go home. Sometimes, when they were on the road, she didn't finish until three or four in the morning. And then she collapsed into bed, too tired to undress. She didn't feel the same thrill that Danny felt standing in front of a crowd, even if she pretended to him that she did. Until it made her so miserable that she could pretend no more.

'First stop – a café,' said Pip peering through the gap in the seats. 'Then Anne Frank's house, then the Van Gogh museum. That okay with you two?'

'Sounds perfect,' said Lara, who had been forced into letting her friends plan the day. But they had planned it knowing what she wanted to see most while they were there.

'I can't believe it. After all these years – three weeks and you'll be Mrs Elmtree,' said Jo. 'It'll take some getting used to, not calling you Lara Cliffe any more. I feel as if I've been Jo England for ever. The days of being Miss Jo Baker seem so long ago now.'

'*If* I get married,' said Lara, without thinking.

'Eh?'

'Nothing,' Lara said quickly.

But Jo wouldn't let it go. 'No, Lara, what do you mean? You can't just pretend you didn't say it.'

'It was a joke.'

'Liar.'

'Last-minute nerves, that's all,' said Lara. 'I keep thinking about what happened last time I was supposed to get married.'

'Last time you were getting married to a dickhead. That's the difference, Lara. There is no way that Freddie would let you down and walk off into the sunset with another woman.'

'I know,' said Lara.

'The man's built you a dressing room and your own bathroom so you can poo in total privacy. That's proper love, that is. Stop worrying,' said Vicky.

Lara smiled. She had no doubt of Freddie's feelings for her. He couldn't wait to be married to her, couldn't wait until she was Mrs Lara Elmtree. And Lara was as giddy as he was about it all. So why was she having all these stupid thoughts about past days and Danny Belfont? And *was* it fate that he was back in her life?

The bus dropped everyone outside the huge central railway station. They were to be back at five o'clock, which left them loads of time to do what they had to.

'Right, the café is over there somewhere,' said Vicky, pointing with one hand while holding her map with the other. 'I'm flipping starving.'

'Tell us something we don't know,' replied Pip. 'I can't understand why you aren't forty stone with all you eat.'

Vicky had a very good appetite, but never put on any weight.

'I do burn it off chasing around after four kids, remember,' she explained. 'Come on – this way, says the map. Look for a sign that says Dam Square.'

They followed her like baby ducklings behind a mama duck across the road, stepping over the many metal tramlines. Then they turned onto a wide, busy street full of shops selling everything from cheese to tulips, chips to clogs.

About halfway down, Vicky halted and nodded to a building on her right. 'What do you think? Should we make a little stop here first?'

The sign above the open doorway said 'SEXMUSEUM'.

'You might pick up some tips for your wedding night,' said Pip, giving Lara a nudge.

'Or give them some tips of your own,' cackled Vicky. 'Come on. Breakfast can wait for half an hour. We can't come to Amsterdam and not go in there.'

Pip attached her selfie stick to her phone and took a photo of them all standing outside and then they went in. It cost five euros each and the woman at the kiosk, who spoke very good English, told them that they were allowed to take as many photos as they wished inside. They took lots. And they giggled like teenage girls who had just found a dirty book on the back seat of a school bus.

Then they left to find the Happy Pancake, which was only a short walk away.

The café was joined to an old church and was

clean and comfortable inside. They all ordered pancakes and coffee, which arrived in record time, delivered by a handsome young waiter.

'I wouldn't mind him with a fried egg,' said Pip with a dirty laugh. She wasn't usually the sort of person to make smutty remarks, so the others looked at her with raised eyebrows.

'What?' she answered their stares.

'Eat your pancake,' ordered Lara. 'Or I'll tell teacher.'

'Funny.'

'We have fast-track tickets, so we don't have to queue at the Anne Frank House,' said Vicky, checking in her handbag yet again to make sure she had brought them. She'd been worried sick about forgetting them.

'How much did they cost?' asked Lara, through a mouthful of pancake. She had cheese on hers. Jo had Nutella, Pip had banana and syrup and Vicky had apple and cinnamon.

'Never mind how much they cost. I told you, Freddie's footing the bill,' said Vicky. 'I tell you, Lara, you haven't half landed on your feet with him.'

'I have to admit, at first I was slightly worried,' said Pip. 'I did think, here she goes again. Another plonker.'

'We all did,' said Vicky with a nod.

Not long after Lara had passed Freddie the salt on the night they met, she went to the loo. Then Freddie tapped Pip on the shoulder and asked her if Lara was single.

'Who's asking?' she said to him, wary of the big, bearded man.

'Me,' he said. 'I'd like to ask her out, so is she ... free?'

'Not to plonkers,' replied Pip, who was on her third glass of wine by then. 'Are you a plonker?'

Freddie had laughed then. 'Sometimes. But I'm a nice plonker.'

'He is the best plonker on the planet,' said the man sitting beside Freddie, turning in his seat to butt in.

'Cheers, pal,' Freddie said to him.

The friend turned to the rest of the table then. 'This lady has asked if Freddie is a plonker. What do we think, lads?'

'He's a great plonker,' said one.

'The best,' said another, and raised his glass as if toasting him.

'You won't find a better plonker than our Freddie,' said another. 'He's the plonker of all plonkers.'

'Lara's coming back,' Jo warned everyone.

Pip sometimes had nightmares in which she'd told Freddie that Lara wasn't single. She was sure that, if she had, Freddie would have respected her answer and not asked her friend out. They would have gone their separate ways and probably never met again. But luckily she said, 'Yes, she is single and her name is Lara. And if you ask her out and mess her around, you'll have us three to deal with. And we can be really scary. Is that understood?'

'Thank you,' said Freddie with a grin. 'I'll let you get on with your meal in peace now.'

Just before the party of men left, Freddie leaned over Lara and asked if he could have a quiet word with her away from everyone. She had no idea what he could want, but still she had followed him to the corner of the room. There he'd told her that he would like to take her out for dinner and had handed over his number written on a scrap of paper. If she didn't text him 'yes', he wouldn't bother her again. If she did, he'd book a table for two at Bistro Marco on Sunday night at seven.

'Bistro Marco?' said Jo and whistled, when Lara told them all what he'd said.

'Bistro Marco?' said Vicky and smiled.

'Bistro Marco?' said Pip, impressed.

Bistro Marco was a very posh Italian on the edge of town.

But Lara had given up on love. She screwed

up his number and put it in the bin at home. Then she remembered how polite he had been, a proper gentleman, and she fished the piece of paper back out. She texted *YES* to the number, met him at Bistro Marco, and here she was, three years later, on her hen do. Her friends loved Freddie, everyone loved Freddie. Even her mother, who'd treated all of her boyfriends as if they were clones of Danny Belfont, adored him. Her parents had finally met the man who was good enough for their daughter. The man who restored her faith in love, years after she thought she had lost it for ever. The man who put the sun back into her heart.

Chapter 6

The House of Anne Frank

They were finishing off their second coffees when a tall youth with long hair, baby-fluff stubble and a denim jacket walked past the table on his way out. It stirred a memory for Jo, who asked, 'Wonder what happened to Danny Belfont.'

Vicky gave her a look of horror. 'Don't you dare mention his name.'

'Haven't you ever been tempted to look him up on the internet, Lara?' asked Pip. 'I've wondered a few times over the years if he ever became the big rock star that he wanted to be.'

'He was a brilliant guitarist, I have to say,' added Jo.

Of course, Lara had looked him up a few times over the years, but should she admit it? She'd never found a mention of him on Google.

'Once or twice.' Lara decided she would admit it. She didn't like lying to her friends. 'No trace. He might have changed his name.'

'What to? Brian May?' said Vicky with a sarcastic tut.

'There aren't many people who don't show up on the internet at all are there?' Jo said. 'That really is the opposite of fame.'

'So we can safely assume he didn't become a household name in the music world,' said Vicky. 'Then again, without you, Lara, it was hardly likely he would.'

'Without me?' Lara laughed. 'What do you mean, without me?'

'Look, let's face it, Lara. He might have had the talent, but he had no drive at all.'

'This trip down memory lane is all well and good, ladies, but we do have a date with Anne Frank and her house. Can we please talk about this later?' cut in Pip, calling over the waiter so they could pay him.

'It's quicker to walk, and then from there we'll catch the hop-on hop-off bus to the Van Gogh Museum,' advised Vicky as they left the Happy Pancake. 'Come on, we'll burn off our pancakes with a stiff stroll.'

'I think I like Amsterdam very much,' said Jo as they followed Vicky through the sunny streets. 'I didn't think there would be that much to do here. Couple of museums and loads of Edam cheese and not much else, but I was totally wrong. It's amazing.'

There was a long queue of people waiting to go into the Anne Frank museum.

'Thank goodness we booked ahead,' said Jo.

'Jed always books ahead,' said Pip. 'Queues bring out the worst in him. He can't wait for anything.'

'Imagine having to sit and wait two and a half years in this house for the war to be over then,' said Lara. 'It must have been terrible for them all. Terrible and scary.'

'They waited all that time and the next year the war would be over. Whoever told the Germans where they were hiding was a proper rotten git,' added Vicky.

They'd all studied Anne Frank's Diary at school, and now they were standing in the actual place where it was written. The large building had been a working factory, so the eight hidden people had to stay deadly silent in the secret annex during the day.

The four hens marvelled at the bookcase that opened like a door and led to the annex. It separated not only two parts of the house, but two complete worlds, one living in a lot more fear than the other. Vicky had to borrow some tissues from Lara when they came to a cabinet with Anne Frank's real red-checked diary in a glass case. She couldn't stop tears leaking out of her eyes.

'Poor girl,' she said. 'I'm going to read that book again with a totally different view now that I've been here and seen where it all happened.'

The living space was larger than they had imagined, but it couldn't have been much fun staying there. They couldn't open the windows or go outside ever, and young Anne had to share her bedroom with a middle-aged man. It must have been like living in a cage, because the annex was no better than a prison. When the four women left the museum and walked out onto the sunny Dutch streets, they were all in serious need of cheering up.

'Makes you think that we should grab life by the balls and live it now, while we can, doesn't it?' said Jo, as they stood waiting for the hop-on hop-off bus to scoop them up and take them to the Van Gogh Museum.

Vicky's fifteen-year-old daughter was the same age as Anne Frank was when she died. 'I think when I get home, I'm going to keep Nia in her bedroom where she will always be safe,' she said.

'Then she might as well be Anne Frank,' replied Pip. 'You have to let her live and enjoy. And hope that she is sensible. You and Adonis have brought her up to be wise about taking stupid risks. We all had a good time and are still here to tell the tale, aren't we?'

'That's what worries me,' said Vicky. 'Remember that week in Benidorm – jet-skis, motorbikes, riding big bananas on the sea? We were mad.'

Pip hooted with laughter. 'Remember the waxwork museum?'

The others burst into laughter then too. That week had been fun, from the moment Jo's dad dropped them off at the airport to the moment he picked them all up again.

'Oh, the waxworks!' said Lara, bending over with a fit of the giggles. 'Wasn't that the funniest place ever?'

'The waxwork of the queen was taller than John Wayne, and looked as if she'd been pulled through a hedge backwards,' added Vicky.

'How many pina coladas had we drunk before we went in?' asked Jo. 'Everything inside that museum seemed so funny.'

'Oh stop, my sides hurt,' said Pip.

'What do you mean, stop – it was you who brought it up. What about David Beckham?' Vicky could hardly get her words out as the memory came rushing to her. 'He looked as if he'd been hit in the face with a frying pan.'

The four of them were bent double as they remembered the flat-faced model of the footballer. The sight of the hop-on hop-off bus coming towards them brought them to their senses. They climbed on, wiping tears of laughter from their faces.

'Next time I come here, I'm going to stay a couple of days and walk everywhere,' said Lara.

'You should come with Freddie,' said Pip. 'I came here with Jed before the kids arrived, and we had a lovely romantic weekend break. We sailed on the canals and had a stroll around the diamond factory and the red light district—'

'Oh, very romantic,' cut in Vicky, making a mental note to try and get some time off to come back here with Adonis. They were so overdue a break for two. Much as she loved her kids, time alone with her Greek hunk was time very well spent.

Chapter 7

Starry Nights and Sunflowers

They had fast-track tickets for the Van Gogh Museum too.

'Wow, this is massive,' said Vicky, looking up at the number of steps there were between floors. 'How many pictures did he do?'

'I think it's nine hundred actual paintings plus a zillion drawings,' said Lara, recalling a TV programme she and Freddie had watched recently. 'And do you know how many he sold in his lifetime?'

'A hundred?' Pip guessed.

'Don't be daft, it has to be more. Two hundred?' said Vicky.

'No, I know this – the answer is one,' said Jo.

'That's a myth, Jo, but the truth is that he hardly sold any. He used to swap some for paints and pencils and even food, sometimes,' Lara answered.

Vicky whistled. 'He could have bought a lot

of pancakes for what they sell for now. How come you know so much about him anyway? I wouldn't have had you down as an art expert.' She nudged her friend playfully.

'Freddie,' explained Lara. 'He's got such a soft spot for old Vincent that he made me into a fan too. He was going to bring me here last year, but I said I didn't fancy it much then.' And she sighed. 'I should have, shouldn't I?'

'Well, you can come with him in the future, can't you?' said Pip.

'Yes, and I will,' replied Lara.

Anyone who judged Freddie by how he looked would never have thought that underneath that rough-looking outer shell was a very gentle soul who enjoyed walking around museums. He watched TV programmes about history and music and read books about art. He might have been a lover of AC/DC and Meatloaf, but that didn't stop him from listening to classical music too. He liked to take a long bath and have Beethoven booming out of the old ghetto blaster he'd had since he was a boy. It was still going strong because Freddie looked after things. And that included Lara. She had never been with anyone who treated her as something valuable, as he did.

'I used to hate going around museums

when we were at school, didn't you?' said Pip. 'Remember that place with all the mummies?' She huffed. 'Seen one, seen 'em all.'

'Yep,' agreed Vicky. 'There were only so many Anglo-Saxon spearheads I could look at without slipping into a coma.'

No one was bored here though. There were floors and floors of paintings, each one a footstep on the path of Vincent's short and tragic life.

'He died at the same age we are now,' said Lara.

'Look at everything he did in his thirty-seven years,' said Vicky. 'He really was a man with some get-up-and-go.'

Lara's thoughts once again strayed to Danny. Vincent Van Gogh could have taught him a thing or two.

The next floor up was much busier than the first one.

'Ah – that explains the crowds and the queues,' said Jo as they came to a large information board. 'The famous *Starry Night* picture is here on loan from New York. We have to see that.'

Vicky, who was very good with her elbows, pushed a way through the people to get to the front, and her friends followed close behind. And there it was: one of the most famous paintings ever. Lara shivered because, whenever she saw it in books or magazines or on the TV, she thought of another starry night sixteen years ago. The night when Danny Belfont proposed to her.

It had been winter and midnight, and the sky above their heads was like a black velvet blanket. It was studded with millions of stars that twinkled like diamonds. The moon was a beautiful silver curve that sat among them like a smile. Lara hadn't been expecting Danny to ask her to marry him. His words made her head so fuzzy that those stars began to spin and blur, until they looked just like they did on Vincent's artwork.

Except ...

As she looked at the lovely painting now, she began to remember something else, something less romantic: how it really was. For a start, it was freezing and that's why all the stars were out: because there was no cloud cover in the sky. And why were they outside when Danny proposed? It came to her then – because they'd had a massive row and she'd walked out of wherever they were into the car park.

She tried to recall where they were in detail. A grotty pub car park. Then she remembered why they'd argued. *Ah yes ...* He'd found the gig, after she had told him that she was sick of getting no help from him in booking places to play. But only a handful of people came because

Danny hadn't sorted out any advertising. So the landlord had refused to pay them. She had told Danny that night that she was done, she was finished. She'd stormed out to the van and he'd followed, tried to talk her round.

'No, Danny, that's it. I'm fed up. I don't want to do this any more.'

'But, babe, I can't do it without you.'

'No. Go solo. It's not for me ...'

'Marry me.'

'What?'

'Marry me.'

And that was the moment when she'd thought she was going to pass out, and looked upwards and saw those stars start to swirl – and not in a good way. And Danny had caught her before she fainted. And the reason she'd nearly passed out was not because she was dizzy with happiness. It was because she hadn't eaten all day, as she'd been too busy trying to do lots of last-minute advertising. Sorting out Danny's mess.

It appeared Vincent Van Gogh's picture of a starry night had unlocked something in her brain that she had painted over, hoping to make a better picture, the way poor artists often did with their canvases.

He didn't buy her a ring, because he couldn't afford one at that time. Then he'd turned up with a new guitar that he told her he'd bought at a rock bottom price. He'd lied, because she found the receipt for it. He could have got her a lovely ring for what he paid for it. She had never told him though. She just kept waiting for the ring he promised to buy for her, but never did.

She'd remembered the story of the starry-night proposal all wrong. She'd told herself it was romantic and perfect, but it hadn't been at all. People said you couldn't lie to yourself, but you could. You could, until something made you face up to the truth.

The four women were all getting crushed in the crowd, so they moved away from the *Starry Night* painting into the next part of the gallery.

'Who does that remind you of?' said Vicky, as they all stood in front of one of Van Gogh's self-portraits.

'Andy Beech,' Pip and Jo answered without even needing to think about it.

'Oh my goodness,' said Lara. In the picture, Vincent had a small pointed chin, hooded eyes, no beard and brushed-back strawberry-blond hair.

'That was another lucky escape you had, Lara,' said Pip, and she shuddered.

'You really have been out with some total idiots,' said Jo, shaking her head.

'I always thought he was so good-looking.' Lara let loose a long sigh.

'He was, Lara, but he was also an animal that you didn't need in your life,' replied Vicky.

Andy Beech had been really nasty underneath his good looks and charm. When he hit Lara in a nightclub, just for talking to Pip's brother, that was the end of that relationship. The slap had hurt less than the shame of everyone witnessing it. Lara chased away the memory by moving on to the next picture: a lovely vase of sunflowers.

'I thought Van Gogh only painted one load of sunflowers, but he painted twelve,' said Pip, reading the information board next to it.

Sunflowers. Freddie had sent her sunflowers the day after they had been to Bistro Marco for the first time. The card read: 'Thank you for bringing some sunshine to my Sunday, love Freddie Elmtree.' The flowers were as sweet as Freddie was. He'd bought her sunflowers every year on the anniversary of the day they met. They were so special to her that she was going to have them everywhere at her wedding. They would be on her cake, in the church and on the bridesmaids' headbands. The men would even be wearing silk sunflowers in their buttonholes. Sunflowers were happy flowers with no rotten memories fastened to them.

Chapter 8

The Bar with the Black Cat

After the museum they caught the bus back into the centre of Amsterdam and did some shopping. They all bought cheese, had their photos taken standing in a pair of giant clogs which were stuck on the ground outside a shop. Pip bought a Dutch hat with long pigtails dangling at the sides.

'Ooh look at you. It's the prat in pigtails all over again,' laughed Lara.

'Your pigtails were a lethal weapon at school,' said Jo. 'Remember, you used to twist your head around really fast and anyone within three feet would get whipped by them.'

'You nearly took Sharon White's eye out once, didn't you? She had to go to nurse because she couldn't see,' said Vicky. 'I never liked her, so I was glad.'

Pip hooted with laughter. 'I'd forgotten all about that. My hair was like a super power at school.' And she turned her head fast from side to side and set the false pigtails spinning. Her friends moved away quickly.

'That looks a nice place. Let's call in here for a Dutch lager, before we get back on the bus,' said Vicky. *Café Van Beeren* said the sign above the tiny bar built on a corner. They piled in with their bags and headed for a free table by the window.

'I like the music,' said Pip, dancing in her chair to an old disco classic. 'Awww, look at the cat.' On the bar was a large black cat sipping from a cup. 'Isn't he lush?'

'Well I'm having an Amstel. It's Dutch and it's beer, so it's a perfect fit,' said Vicky.

'I'll order,' said Pip, 'because I want to stroke the cat.'

Her old cat had died a few months ago and it had really made her sad. She hadn't wanted another because, she said, she didn't want to go through that sort of upset again. Lara watched Pip pet the bar cat, who seemed more than happy to let her. She didn't think it would be too long before Pip rang the local rescue centre, whatever she might say.

'I could stay here for ever,' said Jo, and the others nodded in agreement. Café Van Beeren had such a warm and welcoming vibe. 'I feel as if I've been away for much longer than a night. Why has it taken us so long to have a mini break together?'

'Because life gets in the way of living,' Pip said, putting the first of two lagers down on the table before going back to the bar for the rest.

'Your hen party gave us all the best excuse for a trip,' said Vicky, before taking a long sip of the cold lager and shivering with delight.

'Isn't it nice, Lara, that you've found someone who ticks all the boxes,' smiled Jo at her old friend.

'Not all of them,' Lara smiled back. 'He's not perfect. He snores like a train engine and he burns everything he cooks.'

'If that's the sum of what's wrong with him, I'll swap,' chuckled Vicky, adding quickly, 'Not really. Adonis is a honey.'

Jo held up her glass to toast the bride-to-be.

'Well, Lara, for the first time in your life, you've found someone that we – your best friends – totally approve of. I never thought I'd live to see the day when I said that. Cheers.'

The four of them chinked their glasses together.

'I'm looking forward to your wedding so much,' said Vicky. 'In fact, I think I'm looking forward to it more than I was my own.'

'Yours was a great wedding,' said Pip. 'It made

the big fat Greek wedding in the film look little and thin.'

'It was a smashing day.' Vicky grinned as she slipped back into a warm pool of happy memories. 'I wish I could do it all over again.'

'I enjoyed my wedding day too,' said Jo, who had married Benny in Gretna Green. Just the two of them. She'd had a huge party at home a week later for friends and family. 'We didn't want a fuss and I was never a white dress sort of person.' Jo had always been a tomboy, happiest in jeans and trousers. Dressing up for work was the worst part of her job. She did look regal in her barrister's robe and wig though. Then again, Jo looked classy in Primark shorts and flip-flops.

'Your wedding was the funniest ever, Pip,' said Vicky. 'And you won first prize for best bridesmaids' dresses.'

Pip started to blush. 'Oh please don't.' The dressmaker had made a mistake and cut the necklines far too low.

'If it hadn't been for that dress, I might never have got together with Benny,' said Jo. Benny had been the best man at Pip's wedding. 'He couldn't resist me. He said I looked like a sexy milkmaid.'

'We've had some lovely times together, haven't we?' said Vicky with a wide grin.

'We've been through some bad stuff too,' said Jo. 'I don't know what I would have done without you lot there helping me through when Dad died.' She looked at Lara as she said this. All her friends had been there for her, but it was Lara who'd brought over meals to make sure she ate. She had helped her with the funeral too, because Jo's mum had left when Jo was only a baby. Lara had stayed over at her house when Jo had terrible panic attacks afterwards. For months, Lara had been more of a mum to her than her own mum had ever been.

'Oh, I think you've all helped me more than I've ever helped any of you,' said Lara with a sad smile. She couldn't count how many times she'd cried on their shoulders over the years. 'I only wish I'd had some sense where men were concerned.'

'Me too,' said Vicky. 'I could have bought another restaurant with all the money I've spent on tissues for you.' She gave her a gentle dig with her elbow. 'Only joking. What are friends for?'

'Give her the thing now,' said Jo. 'I think it's the right time.'

'Give her what thing?' asked Lara, eyes zipping from one to the other of them.

Vicky dug deep into her large handbag

and pulled out a gift bag with ducks printed all over it.

'They were the nearest I could find to hens,' she explained, handing it to Lara.

Lara opened the bag to find a book inside. There was a photo of the four of them in their school uniforms on the cover. Lara's mouth opened with glad surprise.

'I can't even remember this pic. When did we have it taken?'

'The day we left school,' said Jo. 'Dad picked us up and took us for a—'

'—burger and chips,' Lara butted in, suddenly recalling it. 'Aw look at us.' Lara had long, dark hair and was sticking out her tongue. Jo was tall, blonde and skinny (she still was). Vicky had short, spiky hair and was holding two fingers up. And Pip looked like a supermodel.

'We had it printed for you. Your mum supplied a few iffy pics, so don't blame only us,' said Pip.

'Oh NO!' cried Lara, staring down at the photo of herself standing with a boy. 'My first boyfriend, Darren Ross. What am I wearing?'

Lara remembered that crop top and how she had taken her very flat tum for granted. Darren Ross was nice but it wasn't really a romance. They were both fourteen and he was her first snog. Lara had wondered what all the fuss was about.

'He's a doctor now,' said Pip. 'He was my consultant when I had the twins. Where do the years go?'

As if the photo had unlocked a door, pictures flooded into Lara's mind of her teenage years. The school discos, her first taste of cider, fancying big John Townsend who everyone fancied. She'd been stunned to find that he fancied her back. They'd had a short but thrilling romance for five weeks. Snogging was *much* better with him.

Lara turned the page to find the year eleven class photo. She pointed out a girl on the front row, a Kendall Jenner lookalike.

'Tina Smith. She stole John Townsend from me,' she said. 'I was gutted.'

'He tried to snog me behind your back,' said Pip.

'And me.' Jo stuck her finger up in the air.

'And me.' So did Vicky. They all burst into laughter.

'We were young then, cutting our teeth on life, making mistakes,' said Lara. She turned the pages to find more happy photos, more happy times. They'd all laughed so much when they were young. She gulped then, finding a picture of a band onstage. Danny Belfont playing his guitar on the left, Lara on the right singing into a mike.

'We weren't sure whether we should put that one in,' said Vicky, 'but we all decided that he was part of your life's journey, so we did.'

'Thank goodness he's in the past.' Jo let a long breath out. 'I do wonder what he's doing now though.'

'Wonder whaaat, he's doing nooow,' sang Vicky and Pip, as if they were in the musical *Grease*.

That reminded Lara of something Vicky had said to her earlier and asked her, 'What did you mean when you said that he had no drive in him?'

'Well he didn't,' replied Vicky. 'If you'd stayed with him, then he might have got somewhere in life, because you both had talent but only you had any drive. Danny Belfont was all mouth and no action. It used to make me so cross, seeing you do all the work while he sat around waiting for everything to land in his lap. He's probably still doing it.'

'It's true,' Pip jumped in. 'Danny was lazy. It was always you booking gigs, Lara, making posters, begging newspapers and radio stations for mentions. You did more than a full-time manager would have done, as well as all the singing.'

'You were the total opposite of him,' added Vicky. 'I mean, look at you, Lara. You didn't just dream about success and do nothing about it. It takes guts to go back to college in your twenties. But you did it. Then you got your degree and started up your own business. You didn't sit around and wait for things to happen. You *made* them happen.'

'I'm just a one-man company though. I only had a little dream—'

'Don't you dare put yourself down, Lara Cliffe,' Jo snapped at her.

'Who the hell said dreams had to be big?' Pip said. 'It doesn't matter what size your dream is, as long as it fits into that dream-sized hole in your heart.' Then she laughed because she didn't realise she could be so poetic.

But Pip was right. Lara had made her dream come true. It hadn't been easy admitting that she'd taken a wrong turn, allowing others to push her onto the wrong path. She might have been good at singing, but she always preferred maths. Numbers interested her. She saw them as puzzles to be solved and enjoyed playing around with them.

So, at twenty-three, she'd taken an A-level course and then went on to university. Four years later she graduated with a first-class honours degree in accounting and finance. Then she set up her own business. Freddie liked to joke with people that he was sleeping with his accountant, and that's why she didn't charge him for her services.

Lara's mother always blamed Danny Belfont for putting Lara off singing, but she'd been wrong. Lara's dreams had nothing to do with music. Nothing at all.

Lara turned the pages in the book to find even more photos of the 'fab four' in various poses with changing hairstyles and figures: fat, thin, brides, pregnant. They'd stuck together through so many shades of light and dark in their lives and they were still together, laughing, and still best mates. Lara dreaded to think where she would have been without their friendship, their support and their kindness. And their love.

Chapter 9

Leaving Amsterdam and Facing the Truth

'It's just turned half-past four,' said Jo, looking at her watch. 'I suggest we start walking back to the bus stop.'

So after a visit to the loo and a goodbye to the barman and the snoozing cat, they left Café Van Beeren for the street outside, which seemed busier than it had before. Lara pictured herself walking here with Freddie. He'd hold her hand because he liked to do that.

Then her brain leapt to a much younger version of herself walking around London with Danny, feeling his long, slim fingers holding tightly on to hers. He pointed out the Albert Hall, told her that one day they'd be playing there. He had such massive dreams. She used to love listening to him telling her how rich they'd be, how famous, how they would tour all over the world. She wanted to be with him to share it. She wanted him to have it all.

On the way back to the ferry she sat next to Pip, who fell asleep before the bus had turned its first corner. Lara took out the book she had bought Freddie from the Van Gogh Museum shop. She flicked through until she found the picture of the *Starry Night* painting. She stared at it hard, and thought of that grubby pub car park and Danny's proposal again.

She'd told Danny she would meet him that night to talk. She didn't have to turn up – after all, he'd let her down enough times. But she knew she would because she needed to cut herself free from him. It was time to finally face the truth – the real truth, and not what she had wanted the truth to be.

Back in their cabin, Vicky and Lara changed out of their T-shirts and into smarter clothes for dinner in the Reef Bistro.

'You all right? You seem a bit quiet,' said Vicky. 'Have we forced too many memories on you today?'

Lara smiled to herself. If only Vicky knew the half of it. She wanted to tell someone about Danny being on the boat, but Vicky was not the best person. She was likely to go hunt him down and throw him overboard. Lara knew she should say nothing, but the secret sat heavy inside her. She was already tired of keeping it.

Lara took a deep breath before owning up. 'Vicky, remember when we were talking about where Danny Belfont is now.'

'I do,' said Vicky, as she stared at herself in the mirror while putting on her mascara.

'I know exactly where he is.'

'Do you? Where is he?'

Here we go, thought Lara. 'He's on this boat.'

Vicky's mouth formed a perfect O before she spoke again. 'Shut. The. Fuck. Up. How do you know?'

'He's a third of Stardust. The group that were onstage last night.'

'The rubbish group?'

'Yes.'

'No way.'

'Yes way.'

'How did you ... What ... Why didn't you tell us?' Vicky put down the mascara. She couldn't focus on her make-up at the moment.

'Well ...' began Lara, not really knowing where to start. 'I mean ... we didn't really look at them, did we? They were just in the background, playing stuff. But you all went to bed and I watched them properly. Then I recognised him.'

'Are you sure? I mean, it's been fifteen years, Lara.'

'The female singer was Sammy King. She was the one who threw up all over the stage. Danny stayed and sang one of his own songs. Trust me, I know it's him.'

'That was *her*? Sammy King?' Vicky huffed. 'So he can stay faithful to someone then?'

'I spoke to him after he came offstage.'

'You did what?' Vicky looked totally stunned.

'He brought me a drink over. For old times' sake.'

'Yeah and I'm Helen Mirren.' Vicky was cross now. 'Lara, it took you years to get him out of your system. Don't let him slip back in two minutes *for old times' sake.*'

Lara sank onto her bed and put her head into her hands. 'It was a shock, Vicky. I can't say it wasn't. My feelings have been all over the place today.'

'Lara, they're just old ghost feelings. Come on, love, we've watched enough of *Most Haunted* to know why ghosts hang around – because of unfinished business. And that is what this is. Ooh, I'll kill him when I see him tonight,' Vicky growled. 'Wait till I tell the others.'

'Please don't,' said Lara quickly. 'I really don't want to ruin everything.'

'Okay, I promise I won't. Not if you don't want me to,' Vicky said, taking hold of her temper. 'But you stay away from him.'

Lara thought she'd better tell her the rest: 'Vic, I said I'd meet him tonight after they'd finished their act.'

Vicky laughed, then realised that Lara wasn't joking. 'Why would you, Lara? What could you possibly have to say to him after all these years?' Vicky shook her head at the thought of her friend and *him* together again. 'I worry about you, mate,' she went on. 'Ever since you went out with Danny, you've let men walk all over you. You weren't like that before, but he changed you somehow. He treated you as second best to his music, and then he left you for someone who wasn't good enough to wipe your shoes. And that's how you've judged yourself ever since.'

'I know,' said Lara. It was true.

'Then along comes lovely Freddie who puts you on a pedestal where you belong, and you shine with him, Lara. You're the person you should be. I don't want you to spoil anything for yourself.'

'I want to say goodbye to a past I've never been quite able to let go of before I marry Freddie,' said Lara. 'I know what I'm doing.'

'For your sake, Lara, I really hope you do,' said Vicky, picking up her lipstick.

Lara hoped she did too, because she had an awful habit of believing lies, even ones she told to herself.

Part III

Rotterdam to Hull

Chapter 10

Dinner Before Danny

'Great. They're expecting high winds again,' said Pip, hearing the people on the next table talking to the waiter in the Reef Bistro. 'I hope I can get to sleep.'

'I hope you don't sleep like you did last night,' Jo said to her. 'You snored like a pig with a blocked nose.'

'I think that singing group in the Jolly Sailor bar bored me so much that I blacked out. Look, I'm yawning now at the thought of them. What were they called? Snowstorm, Stardrops?'

'Starburst, wasn't it?' suggested Jo. 'Or was it Sunstroke?'

'Well, maybe we should try the other bar tonight,' said Vicky.

'Ooh yes, the Moonlight bar. I'm up for that,' replied Lara.

She and Vicky had decided to steer the others away from the Jolly Sailor because they would not have been able to act normally when Stardust came on. This would only lead to Pip and Jo working out that something was not right. Their only option was to totally stay clear of the place.

'Isn't it funny how you can be totally full after a starter and a main course, and yet always have room for pudding,' said Jo, looking at the dessert menu. 'I have no idea what to have. I could eat everything on this list.'

'I'm not a lover of brownies, so that's a no,' said Pip with a sniff. 'You can't go wrong with a cheesecake, so I'm having that again. It was lovely last night.'

'Freddie makes a nice cheesecake,' said Lara. 'So long as a recipe doesn't involve an oven, he's quite good at cooking.'

An unwelcome picture appeared in her head of Danny watching her eat a pudding. '*You shouldn't be eating stuff like that. You'll get fat. You won't look good onstage.*'

'Freddie enjoys his food, you can tell,' said Vicky. 'So does Adonis. If he didn't go running, he'd be the size of Corfu.'

'Freddie does weights. We're having a keep-fit room in the new house,' said Lara.

The others trilled 'Oooh' at her.

'Did that sound as if I was bragging? Sorry.'

'You brag as much as you like,' Vicky said with a smile. 'I think it's great that you're going to live in a big house. And then you should have babies. There's far too much room in your new home for only two people.'

'You'll have to get a move on,' put in Pip. 'You'll be forty in two and a half years. Your eggs will be drying up soon.'

'Oh please.' Jo pulled a face, putting down her menu. 'I think I'll pass on the egg custard tart. Cheesecake for me too. And a coffee to follow.' She sat back in the chair and grinned. 'I've had such a lovely time. A nice quiet hen party for a change.'

'Who had the noisiest hen party?' asked Lara.

'Vicky – by far,' Jo and Pip agreed at the same time. Twenty girls had gone to Cyprus for five days and hardly slept at all.

'It would have been unforgettable if any of us could remember it,' Vicky laughed. 'At least the photos proved we had a good time.'

'We need to get away once a year, even if it's just overnight in a spa. It's been wonderful. I can't remember the last time we all did something together like this,' said Pip.

'It was my thirty-third birthday,' said Vicky, who was the youngest of them. 'We had a day in Alton Towers and stayed over at the hotel.'

Lara remembered it too well. She and Andy Beech had not long broken up and she'd had a puffed-up cheek and a black eye that make-up wouldn't cover. She'd felt as battered inside as out.

After the cheesecakes and the coffees, they went over to the Moonlight bar. They had to pass the Jolly Sailor to get to it and the band was playing. Lara's nerves felt as tight as harp strings.

'They sound as bad tonight as they did last night,' said Pip.

'I couldn't sit and listen to them again. I might do something I regret,' said Vicky, through clenched teeth. Lara read a meaning in her words that escaped the others.

No sooner had they sat down with their drinks than Pip started to yawn. 'Sorry,' she said. 'I took a seasickness tablet right before dinner. I didn't think it'd make me drowsy so soon.'

Then Vicky yawned and said, 'Oh no, it's catching.'

'We're getting old,' Jo laughed.

'Speak for yourself. My life is just starting,' said Lara.

'Yes, so don't do anything to mess it up,' Vicky said, giving her a kick under the table.

'I think it's so romantic what happened between you and Freddie,' said Pip. 'But just think, if there'd been a salt pot on his table and he hadn't turned around to ask for ours, your paths wouldn't have crossed, Lara.'

'Then again, she might have bumped into Keanu Reeves on a trip to London and be marrying him instead,' said Jo. 'Who knows what's around the corner?'

'Yes, who knows what's around the corner,' repeated Vicky, her words carrying a punch because she and Lara knew what was around it. Or rather – who.

'Good job we were in a rubbish Greek place where they forget to put salt pots on tables,' said Pip, and winked at Vicky. Fate really was a strange thing, they all agreed on that.

Ten minutes later, Pip could not keep her eyes open and asked if anyone minded if she went to bed.

'Don't be silly, just go,' said Lara. 'I'm tired too.' It was a lie. She was wide awake but faked a yawn.

'In that case, I think I'll tag along with you, Pip,' said Jo. 'And I'll have one of your seasickness tablets, if you have one to spare. I'm okay at the moment, but if the sea gets as bumpy as it did last night, I might have a problem.'

'Well that was easy, getting rid of those two,' said Vicky, waving them off with a cheery *Goodnight, see you in the morning.* 'Now you've only got me to lose, Lara, before you hook up with Danny *Bellend*.'

Lara didn't want to admit to Vicky that she was getting more nervous by the minute about meeting Danny again. She felt as if she didn't want to, but had to. She also thought she knew why that was.

'I promise you, I won't be talking through the night with him,' she said.

'I'd stand him up, if I were you – teach him a lesson – but I know you won't,' said Vicky. 'I wish I could be a fly on the wall. Or a bee, then I could swoop down and sting the bas—'

'Behave, Vicky Floros,' Lara cut her off before the swear word. 'I'm not going to do anything silly like run off with him.'

'Promise?'

Lara made a cross sign on her chest where her heart sat.

'I promise. Don't worry.'

'I am worrying,' said Vicky, 'and I'll tell you why: because I know how much you loved Danny Belfont. And I know how long it took you to get over him. In fact, until you met Freddie, I wasn't sure you ever had. And now I'm back to wondering that same thing.' Vicky gave her friend a smile. 'We all care so much about you, Lara. And I don't want Danny Belfont messing up any more of your life. Not now, not when you are about to marry someone who loves you properly.'

She rubbed her forehead as if trying to rid it of a pain. 'I can't tell you what to do, Lara, you're a grown woman, but I can tell you – as someone who thinks the world of you – to be careful. If the Danny Belfont of today is anything like the Danny Belfont of yesterday, he will be dripping in charm that smells like honey, but it'll taste like bullshit. Be warned.' And with that she downed the rest of her drink. 'Come on, I'll walk with you to the Jolly Sailor.'

Chapter 11

The Truth about Danny

The table they had all sat at the previous night in the Jolly Sailor was taken, but there was a free one in the corner for two people. Lara and Vicky sat down and listened to Sammy King murdering 'Locomotion'.

'She's no Kylie, is she?' said Vicky, studying her. 'I wouldn't have recognised her in a million years if you hadn't told me it was her.'

They'd all known Sammy King from school, even though she was in the year below. She'd been Samantha then. They'd had a fit of the giggles at a school speech day once when she'd won an award for effort, and the head had read out her full name – Samantha Ethel Gladys King. Thinking back, it had been Mr Fenton who whispered to them that, if they didn't get control of themselves, they would be marched out of the hall. Pip's lip had bled, because she'd had to bite down on it so hard to stop laughing. Lara burst into a chuckle at the memory.

'What's up?' asked Vicky.

'Samantha Ethel Gladys King, that's what,' said Lara, and that set Vicky off.

'Do you remember Mr Fenton telling us off for laughing about it?' said Vicky. 'I think we were the only four girls in the whole school that didn't fancy him. Isn't it odd that one of us went and married him?'

'Oh more than odd, much more. Even Pip thinks it's odd.'

Vicky's laughter died down as her eyes shifted from Sammy King to Danny Belfont.

'What is he doing with his life?' she asked, with a puzzled shake of her head. 'I might hate his guts, but he's so much better than what he's doing now.'

'Locomotion' ended and there were a few pitiful claps.

'And now for our last song ...' began Sammy, as someone heckled her from the crowd and said, 'Thank goodness'. She ignored it and carried on: '"The Wind Beneath My Wings".'

'I love this song – I can't listen to her destroying it, so I'll leave you, Lara,' said Vicky. She leaned over and gave her friend a kiss on the cheek. 'Be careful,' she said sternly. 'And don't forget who the wind beneath your wings is, okay?' And with that she was gone.

Lara listened to the song, taking in the lyrics. It was about a person who put someone else's happiness before their own because they loved them so much. She suddenly felt very sad.

Danny started to play a short guitar solo, his fingers moving expertly over the strings, making it look so easy. He'd once told her that he couldn't remember a time before he could play. All he had ever wanted to do was be a guitarist. The best in the world.

Sammy began to sing again and Lara was reminded of something her mother once said – *Couldn't hold a tune even with superglue and a sticky rope.* Lara tried to think when she'd said it, and then remembered that it was at her parents' golden wedding celebrations last year. They'd had a karaoke, and Freddie and her dad had got up to do it as a duet. 'YOU are the wind beneath my wings,' Freddie had sung at her, even though it was more of a growl which prompted her mum's laughing comment.

She had been over six months single when she met Freddie. She was raw and bruised and felt as if she was made only of tears, and that, when all of them had been cried, there would be nothing left of her. She had decided she would never go out with another man ever. Being alone for the rest of her life was better than making the same mistakes over and over again. She was done, finished with trying to find love. It was only when she met Freddie that she found out that true love was *two* people putting the other first, not just one.

More clapping from the crowd as Sammy bowed and said, 'Thank you, everyone, and goodnight from Paul, our drummer, Daniel, our guitarist, and from me, Sammy. We've been Stardust.'

Lara looked at her watch. She was five minutes away from an important moment in her life. Maybe the most important one ever.

Ten minutes later, Danny still hadn't arrived. Lara glanced at her watch and decided that she'd give him another five. Another five came and went. Wouldn't that be funny, if he stood her up yet again, she thought, with a heavy heart. She was about to leave when she spotted him walking towards her with two white wines.

'Sorry,' he said. 'I couldn't get away.'

Lara wondered what excuse he had made to Sammy, what lie he had told her, because she knew that he wouldn't have said that he was going to have a drink with his ex-fiancée and talk about fate.

'Had a good day?' He smiled at her as he sat down.

'We had an amazing day,' she replied.

'Oh, Lara, I haven't been able to get you out of my head,' said Danny then. 'I've had a rush of memories all about you. Things I haven't thought of for years came flooding back to me.'

Lara stopped herself just in time from telling him that the same had happened to her.

'Well, we can't change what happened in the past, can we?' she said, feeling proud that she sounded so grown-up and wise.

'No,' Danny said, 'but we can change the path we're on now, the future we're heading to. You've made me think about my life so much, Lara. I feel as if I've been plugged into an electric socket and I've got energy in my heart. It's fate that we met again. It has to be.'

This was the sort of thing that Vicky had told her to watch out for, the bullshit. But her old friend had no need to worry.

'I'm glad I've had that effect on you,' Lara said. 'And maybe it is fate that we met again, Danny. Maybe me being here was meant to shake you up, and make you realise that you should be doing something better than what you are. Your dreams were as big as your talent, so what happened?'

'You left,' said Danny. 'That's what happened.'

'I didn't. You replaced me. I wasn't *the girl that got away*, as in your song last night. I was the girl who got pushed out.' Lara couldn't believe she was saying this and staying calm.

'You threw away your talent,' said Danny.

'I hated singing onstage,' said Lara.

'No you didn't, you loved it.'

'No, Danny, I hated it. I hated everything about it. I hated touring, having to set up and pack away, and running through the songs over and over again. I hated learning lyrics and not getting home until long past midnight. Just because you're good at something doesn't mean you have to like doing it.'

'I suppose you're happy now, doing sums in an office,' Danny scoffed.

'Yes, I am,' said Lara, meaning it. She was happy. She felt fulfilled and content, and work didn't feel like work because she enjoyed doing what she did. 'For your sake, I tried to pretend that your dream was mine too, but it wasn't. And that was the only glue holding us together.'

'How can you say that, Lara? We loved each other. I asked you to marry me,' Danny protested.

'You asked me to marry you to stop me leaving the group. That was the only reason.'

89

And there it was – the truth that had found its way to her that day. Vincent Van Gogh's lovely pictures of stars and sunflowers had shown her what she hadn't really been able to see before. What she hadn't wanted to see before.

'And then you got together with Sammy so you wouldn't have to marry me,' she carried on. 'You never loved me, Danny. You loved my voice and the music we made together, but you didn't love *me*. And once I'd told you that I *really* didn't want to sing any more, I was of no use to you, so you moved on.'

'I did love you,' said Danny, but there was little force in his protest. 'I never stopped loving you. That's why I wrote that song about the girl that got away.'

'You're stamping a truth over a lie, Danny. Just as I have been for years. I think deep down some sensible part of me saw things as they really were, and that I had to let you go. Whatever we had wasn't love, even if we thought it was at the time. Not true love. Not like I have now with my Freddie. His dreams really are the ones I want to share. And our dreams might sound really small and boring compared with filling the Albert Hall, but we are living them. And life is great.'

Lara got up from the chair. She hadn't touched

the wine he'd bought. It stood there as yet another symbol of how far apart they were. The Lara who drank white wine was long gone, the Lara who drank red was here and now.

She leaned over, planted a kiss on his cheek. 'Goodbye, Danny. Don't look for what you need in other people, look for it in yourself. Because it's there, trust me. It's never too late to try and be who you always wanted to be. Good luck.'

The boat bounced on a wave and a loud creak came from somewhere. It sounded like something breaking. It sounded as if that connection between Lara and the past had snapped at last and set her free.

Vicky was sitting up in bed reading when Lara came in. She dropped her book and stared at her friend, waiting for her to begin talking.

'So?' she prompted when Lara stayed silent.

Lara smiled and that confused Vicky even more.

'Guess what I realised today,' she said. 'That Danny Belfont never loved me at all.' She was smiling but tears were dropping from her eyes at the same time.

Vicky's face crumpled with sympathy. 'Oh he did, Lara. I know—'

'No, he didn't, but it's fine,' said Lara, cutting

her off. 'I'm sure he liked me. But love ... I don't think so. That's why I was so easy to replace when Sammy King came along with her big hopes of being a megastar.' She flicked some tears away from her cheeks. 'I could have insisted she leave, but I didn't. He had more chance of living out his dreams of stardom with her than with me.'

Vicky huffed. 'That worked out well for them both then didn't it?'

Lara gave a soft chuckle but tears were still raining from her eyes. 'I must have known in my heart that he didn't love me; that's why I gave him the chance to let me go.'

'And the git took it and ran with it.'

'Yes.'

Vicky opened up the bag at the side of her, hunted inside it for her tissues and then handed them to Lara.

'I know you loved him a lot, Lara, so that can't have been an easy thing to find out.'

'He said that fate had made us meet again and I'm sure he was right, but not for the obvious reasons. I think I needed to face some hard facts about what true love is and what it isn't. And I think fate wanted to give Danny a kick up the backside.'

'Thank goodness.' Vicky blew out two cheeks

full of air. 'I thought you were going to say that fate wanted to put you together again.'

'No. Fate wants us to stay totally away from each other.' Lara blew her nose, her tears were done with now. 'You know, I love music, I love to sing in the bath and around the house and in the car with Freddie doing silly duets, but . . . I'm so much happier adding up numbers at a desk than I ever was performing on a stage.'

Lara sat down on her bed. 'Sometimes I used to wonder if I'd done the right thing turning my back on stardom, because so many people told me I should sing and I shouldn't waste what I could do with my voice. I used to feel so bad that I'd let Danny down, and that he might have filled the Albert Hall if I'd hung on in there and helped him. But I had to live *my* dream, not his, not anyone else's. Now I see that, I feel totally free. Does that make sense?'

'Perfect sense.'

'All these years, I've been fooling myself that Danny loved me because it would hurt too much to think that he never did and he was just using me to make his own dreams come true.'

'Time to put the past to bed, mate. Say a last goodbye to it, and a big fat hello to a fab future with Freddie. You're going to have such a great life with him.'

'I know and I can't wait.'

Vicky grinned. 'So, just to confirm – so I can stop worrying and sleep – you have no plans at all to join Stardust?'

Lara grinned back at her and put her hand on her heart. 'None,' she said.

Part IV

Amsterdam

Chapter 12

What Happened Next

Freddie Elmtree and his wife of a year were in Amsterdam, and the day was as warm and sunny as it had been the last time she had been there with her hens. They'd had pancakes and coffee in the Happy Pancake café, next to the church in Dam Square. Then they had walked to Anne Frank's house and it had moved Lara even more than it had the first time. Freddie had left the museum wiping his eyes too, but he was never ashamed about showing his feelings. Now they were standing in front of a painting of sunflowers in the Vincent Van Gogh museum. They were the happiest of flowers for Lara because they always reminded her of her husband. Sunflowers and Freddie, both big, bright and lovely, and the sight of them filled Mrs Elmtree's heart with cheer.

'Isn't that lovely?' said Freddie. 'I've always wanted to see the real thing and now I have, so that's another box ticked.'

They'd seen the *Starry Night* painting together too. It was back in its home in New York and they'd visited it at Christmas. Now whenever Lara saw pictures of it, she thought of their wonderful, loved-up holiday and Freddie's thrilled face. All other memories, which had been fastened to that painting before, had faded away to nothing.

Their wedding had been full of sunflowers: in the church, on the cake, on suit lapels, in the bridesmaids' headbands – everywhere. It was their lucky flower. And thanks to Vincent Van Gogh's paintings, Lara had found a release from a burden of sadness and regret that she had been carrying around with her like a rock for fifteen long years. Mr Van Gogh would always be her favourite artist for that. If, one day, she ever bumped into him in heaven, she would buy him a very large red wine.

On the boat, Tony and the Tones had been playing in the Jolly Sailor bar, not Stardust. She'd typed Danny's name into Google only once – the week before they sailed – and found that he had a website now. There was a video recording on the home page of him playing 'The Girl That Got Away'. She didn't listen to it. She wished him well, hoped he had finally started to stretch his hand out to reach for his own big, shiny star without waiting for someone else to hook it down for him. He was no more to her now than someone she used to know, part of a past that belonged in the past. She wouldn't google him again.

'What do you think about painting the nursery bright yellow?' asked Freddie. The idea just came to him while he was studying the flowers. 'And hanging some of Vincent's pictures in it, for luck. Not the real ones, obvs, as I'm a few million quid short, but I'm working on it.' He laughed then, a huge rumble of a sound that made Lara smile as her hand came to rest on her four-month bump.

'I think that's a brilliant idea, Mr Elmtree,' she said.

About Quick Reads

*"Reading is such an important
building block for success"*
– Jojo Moyes

Quick Reads are short books written by
best-selling authors. They are perfect for regular
readers and adults reading for pleasure for
the first time. Since 2006, over 4.8 million copies
of more than 100 titles have been read!

Available to buy in paperback or ebook and to
borrow from your local library.

Turn over to find your next Quick Read ...

A special thank you to Jojo Moyes
for her generous donation and support of Quick Reads
and to **Here Design**.

Quick Reads is part of The Reading Agency, a national
charity tackling life's big challenges through
the proven power of reading.

www.readingagency.org.uk
@readingagency   #QuickReads

The Reading Agency Ltd. Registered number: 3904882 (England & Wales)
Registered charity number: 1085443 (England & Wales)
Registered Office: Free Word Centre, 60 Farringdon Road, London, EC1R 3GA
The Reading Agency is supported using public funding by Arts Council England.

Supported using public funding by
**ARTS COUNCIL
ENGLAND**

THE READING AGENCY

Find your next Quick Read: the 2020 series

More from Quick Reads

For a complete list of titles and more information
on the authors and stories visit

www.readingagency.org.uk/quickreads

Continue your reading journey

The Reading Agency is here to help keep you
and your family reading:

Challenge yourself to complete six reads
by taking part in **Reading Ahead**
at your local library, college or workplace
readingahead.org.uk

Join **Reading Groups for Everyone** to find a
reading group and discover new books
readinggroups.org.uk

Celebrate reading on **World Book Night**
every year on 23 April
worldbooknight.org

Read with your family as part of the
Summer Reading Challenge
at your local library
summerreadingchallenge.org.uk

For more information, please visit our website:
readingagency.org.uk

Milly Johnson

My One True North

**Laurie and Pete should never have met.
But fate has pushed them together for a reason.**

Six months ago, on the same night, **Laurie**
and **Pete** both lost their partners. Struggling
to manage the grief, they join the same
counselling group – and meet each other.

From their sadness, Pete and Laurie find happiness
growing and they sense a fresh new beginning.
Except, the more they talk, the more Laurie begins
to spot the strange parallels in their stories.

Then Pete discovers a truth that changes everything.

But, as surely as a compass points north,
some people cannot be kept apart.

My One True North is a story of friendship
and what love means, of secrets uncovered,
teashops on corners and the northern lights.

**'Every time you discover a new Milly book,
it's like finding a pot of gold'** *heat*

AVAILABLE FOR PRE-ORDER NOW

SIMON &
SCHUSTER

Have you read them all?

All of Milly's books are available in print and eBook, and are available to download in eAudio